Adventures with The King™

A HERO'S PRAYER

BY
SHERI ROSE SHEPHERD

ILLUSTRATED BY
JENNIFER ZIVOIN

TYNDALE

Tyndale House Publishers, Inc.
Carol Stream, Illinois

FOCUS ON THE FAMILY®

A Focus on the Family book published by Tyndale House Publishers, Inc., Carol Stream, Illinois 60188

Focus on the Family and the accompanying logo and design are federally registered trademarks of Focus on the Family, 8605 Explorer Drive, Colorado Springs, CO 80920.

TYNDALE and Tyndale's quill logo are registered trademarks of Tyndale House Publishers, Inc.

Book Design by Josh Lewis
Text set in Mrs Eaves XL.

For manufacturing information regarding this product, please call 1-800-323-9400.

For information about special discounts for bulk purchases, please contact Tyndale House Publishers at csresponse@tyndale.com, or call 1-800-323-9400.

ISBN 978-1-58997-985-7

Printed in Malaysia

25   24   23   22   21   20   19
7   6   5   4   3   2   1

There once was a boy named Carter.
He had an amazing imagination.

At bedtime, Carter would fall asleep and dream about heroes with superpowers. And sometimes he dreamed about having superpowers, too.

Carter would fly through the air, rising up from his room, his house, and his neighborhood. Soon he was flying above the city, zipping around tall buildings and saving people from danger.

"Guess what I dreamed about last night?" asked Carter.

Mama paused from sipping her coffee. "Hmmm, let's see. How many people did you rescue?"

"Just one this time," Carter said. "I was flying over a baseball field and found a lost lady there. She looked like Grandma. So I flew her home."

Mama smiled. "I'm sure she was happy about that!"

Then Mama looked into Carter's eyes and asked, "Son, if you could have superpowers, what would they be?" Carter thought for a minute.

Then he replied, "I want to fly so I can rescue people. I want to be super strong so I can carry broken-down cars to the gas station. And I want to be invisible!"

Mama looked at the clock. "Can you be my hero and put
the dishes away? We need to leave soon."

When they arrived at school, Carter said,
"Mama, I want to pray that I can be a hero today."

Mama agreed, and before she had time to close her eyes,
Carter prayed a hero prayer. "Dear God, Thank you for
school and my friends and playtime, and please, I want
to be a hero. Can you make me one? I want to fly, be
super strong, and invisible! Amen."

Carter waved good-bye to mama. He couldn't
wait to play superheroes with his friends!

After school, Mama and Carter went to the grocery store. They didn't need much and soon wheeled over to the check-out lane.

In line behind them, a family unloaded their groceries. The father looked very nervous. He pulled out his wallet and looked at the money inside. Then he said, "I'm sorry, kids, but we have to put some things back."

"You can take back my favorite snacks, Daddy," the girl offered. The dad took her bag of snacks, along with a few other items, and said he would be right back.

Carter looked at Mama and whispered, "That girl just gave back the same snacks I have. I want to give her my snacks." Mama paid for the snacks, and Carter gave the bag to the girl. Then Mama and Carter quickly left the store.

Mama looked at Carter as he helped load the car. She said, "You know what? I think God answered your prayer to be a superhero. You just used your superpower to be invisible!"

"What do you mean, Mama?" asked Carter.
"I wasn't invisible!"

"Oh yes, you were. You gave that girl your snacks and no one else knew about it."

"Do you think God saw?" asked Carter.

"God sees everything," replied Mama. "And He works in invisible ways sometimes, too. Today that girl got to see the invisible hand of God because you gave her your snacks."

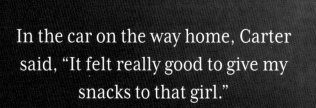

In the car on the way home, Carter said, "It felt really good to give my snacks to that girl."

"True heroes have a heart like God's," said Mama. "They look out for people. They try to make the world a better place."

That night during supper, Carter said, "I had fun using my invisible superpowers today!"

Mama explained, "Son, you have something better than superpowers. You have the heart of a hero, and that is more powerful than flying, strength, or being invisible."

Carter smiled deep down to his toes. And then he raced away . . . to play superheroes, of course!

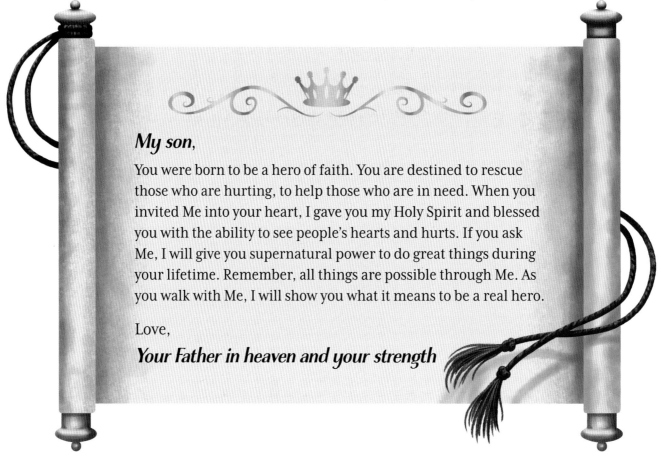

My son,

You were born to be a hero of faith. You are destined to rescue those who are hurting, to help those who are in need. When you invited Me into your heart, I gave you my Holy Spirit and blessed you with the ability to see people's hearts and hurts. If you ask Me, I will give you supernatural power to do great things during your lifetime. Remember, all things are possible through Me. As you walk with Me, I will show you what it means to be a real hero.

Love,

Your Father in heaven and your strength

TREASURE OF TRUTH

"Lord, when did we ever see you hungry and feed you? Or thirsty and give you something to drink?" And the King will say, "I tell you the truth, when you did it to one of the least of these my brothers and sisters, you were doing it to me."

Matthew 25:37, 40